WHAT WOULD JESUS DO?

BARBOUR
PUBLISHING, INC.
Uhrichsville, Ohio

© MCMXCVIII by Barbour Publishing, Inc.

ISBN 1-57748-294-8

All Scripture quotations are taken from the Authorized King James Version of the Bible.

Published by Barbour Publishing, Inc., P.O. Box 719, Uhrichsville, Ohio 44683
http://www.barbourbooks.com

Member of the
Evangelical Christian
Publishers Association

Printed in the United States of America.

 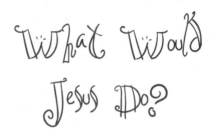

What Would Jesus Do?

What would you do in a certain situation? What would Jesus do? The answer might not always be the same. It always comes down to WWJD. Jesus will never steer you wrong.

With its emphasis on developing a Christlike mind-set, WWJD is the latest craze for Christian teenagers. But did you know that it all started when your great-great-grandparents were your age?

WWJD is the focus of Charles M. Sheldon's classic 1896 novel *In His Steps*, about a pastor who shakes up his congregation, and his entire community, by pledging to ask "What would Jesus do?" before making any decisions, however large or small. It was a good idea a century ago, and it's still a good idea today.

You're already familiar with WWJD. Now, get to know *In His Steps*. This book includes passages from the book, corresponding verses from the Bible, and prayers—all will help you determine "What would Jesus do?"

So now, what will you do?

If any man will come after me, let him deny himself, and take up his

cross daily, and follow me. Luke 9:23

"What do you mean when you sing 'I'll go with Him, with Him, all the

way?' Do you mean that you are suffering and denying yourselves and

trying to save lost, suffering humanity just as I understand Jesus did?"

from *In His Steps*

Dear Jesus, help me pick up my cross today and follow You.

"We must offer the Lord whatever interior sacrifice we are able to give Him. . .even though our actions may in themselves be trivial."

—Teresa of Avila

This is my commandment, That ye love one another, as I have loved you. John 15:12

"It seems to me there's an awful lot of trouble in the world that somehow wouldn't exist if all the people who sing such songs went and lived them out."

from *In His Steps*

· ·

Father, help me to
live out Your love.

· ·

"Love doesn't just sit there like a stone,

it has to be made, like bread."

—Ursula K. LeGuin

Greater love hath no man than this, that a man lay down his life for his friends. Ye are my friends, if ye do whatsoever I command you.   John 15:13–14

"You have been good to me. Somehow I feel as if it was what Jesus would do."

from *In His Steps*

Help me, Jesus,
to be like You.

"The way of Christ is not possible without Christ."

—William Russell Maltby

For even hereunto were ye called: because Christ also suffered for us, leaving us an example, that ye should follow his steps. 1 Peter 2:21

"I want volunteers from the First Church who will pledge themselves, earnestly and honestly for an entire year, not to do anything without first asking the question, 'What would Jesus do?' And after asking that question, each one will follow Jesus as exactly as he knows how, no matter what the result may be."

from *In His Steps*

· ·

In each thing that happens
today, Lord, show me what
You would do.

· ·

"We cannot separate His demands from His love.

We cannot dissect Jesus and relate only to the

parts that we like."

—Rebecca Manley Pippert

Be ye therefore followers of God, as dear children; And walk in love, as Christ also hath loved us, and hath given himself for us an offering and a sacrifice to God. Ephesians 5:1-2

"Our motto will be, 'What would Jesus do?' Our aim will be to act just as He would if He was in our places, regardless of immediate results."

from *In His Steps*

Dear Lord, let me act today the way You would if You were in my place. I want to be God's follower, His dear child.

"If we do not cling to riches, selfishness or greed—then

I believe we are getting closer to God."

—Daniel Ortega

If any of you lack wisdom, let him ask of God, that giveth to all men liberally, and upbraideth not; and it shall be given him.   James 1:5

"I am a little in doubt as to the source of our knowledge concerning what Jesus would do. Who is to decide for me just what He would do in my case? It is a different age. There are many perplexing questions in our civilization that are not mentioned in the teachings of Jesus. How am I going to tell what He would do?"

from *In His Steps*

I need Your wisdom, God. My life seems so confusing. Please show me what You want me to do.

"Don't worry about what you do not understand. . . .

Worry about what you do understand [in the Bible]

but do not live by."

—Corrie ten Boom

Thy word is a lamp unto my feet,

and a light unto my path.

Psalm 119:105

"There is no way that I know of," replied the pastor, "except as we study Jesus through the medium of the Holy Spirit. You remember what Christ said speaking to His disciples about the Holy Spirit: 'Howbeit when He the spirit of truth is come, He shall guide you into all the truth; for He shall not speak from Himself; but what things soever He shall hear, there shall He speak; and He shall declare unto you the things that are to come. He shall glorify me; for He shall take of mine and declare it unto you. All things whatsoever the Father hath are mine; therefore said I, that He taketh of mine and shall declare it unto you.' There is no other test that I know of."

from *In His Steps*

Shine Your light,
Christ Jesus,
on my path.

"God cannot reveal anything to us

if we have not His spirit."

—Oswald Chambers

Then spake Jesus again unto them, saying, I am the light of the world: he that followeth me shall not walk in darkness, but shall have the light of life.

John 8:12

"But when it comes to a genuine, honest, enlightened following of Jesus' steps, I cannot believe there will be any confusion either in our own minds or in the judgment of others."

from *In His Steps*

I don't want to walk
in the dark, Lord Jesus.
I want Your Spirit's light
to fill my life.

"Decisions which are made in the light of

God's Word are stable and show wisdom."

—Vonette Z. Bright

Master, I will follow thee whithersoever thou goest. Matthew 8:19

"After we have asked the Spirit to tell us what Jesus would do and have

received an answer to it, we are to act regardless of the results to ourselves."

from *In His Steps*

Take my fears, Jesus, take my worries. Take everything that holds me back from following You.

"Let nothing deter you. . .remember it is God who has called you and it is the same as when He called Moses or Samuel."

—Gladys Aylward

The day following Jesus would go forth into Galilee, and

findeth Philip, and saith unto him, Follow me.   John 1:43

"I believe Mr. Maxwell was right when he said we must

each one of us decide according to the judgment we feel

for ourselves to be Christlike."

from *In His Steps*

Jesus, help me keep my eyes on You. Remind me not to worry about what others are doing. Keep me focused.

"The search for God is, indeed, an entirely personal under-

taking. . .the most audacious adventure that one can dare."

—Alexis Carrel

Judge not, and ye shall not be judged: condemn not,

and ye shall not be condemned: forgive,

and ye shall be forgiven.

Luke 6:37

"I judge no one else; I simply decide

my own course."

from *In His Steps*

Forgive me for the times I've judged others, Lord. Help me to pray for them instead, while I concentrate on keeping my own behavior in line with Your love.

"Forbear to judge, for we are sinners all."

–William Shakespeare

I am come a light into the world, that whosoever believeth on me

should not abide in darkness. John 12:46

"Who were these people? They were immortal souls. What was

Christianity? A calling of sinners, not the righteous, to repentance."

from *In His Steps*

Thank You, Lord Jesus, for lighting my darkness. Thank You for loving me when I was still your enemy. Thank You for calling me.

"We think we must climb to a certain height of goodness before we can reach God. But. . .if we are in a hole the Way begins in the hole. The moment we set our face in the same direction as His, we are walking with God."

—Helen Wodehouse

[Jesus] saith unto them, They that are whole have no need of the physician, but they that are sick: I came not to call the righteous, but sinners to repentance.   Mark 2:17

"It is easy to love an individual sinner, especially if he is personally picturesque or interesting. To love a multitude of sinners is distinctively a Christlike quality."

from *In His Steps*

Fill me, Jesus,
with Your love. Let me
show that love to the world
in concrete ways.

"Non-Christians and Christians both do social work,

but non-Christians do it for something while we do

it for Someone."

—Mother Teresa

Be kindly affectioned one to another with brotherly love; in honour preferring one another; Not slothful in business; fervent in spirit; serving the Lord. Romans 12:10–11

"I am absolutely convinced that Jesus in my place would be absolutely unselfish. He would love all these men in His employ. He would consider the main purpose of all the business to be a mutual helpfulness, and would conduct it all so that God's kingdom would be evidently the first object sought."

from *In His Steps*

Show me, dear God, the places where I'm selfish. I know my vision is full of blind spots. Shine Your Spirit's light into all the dark corners of my heart.

"When we turn *to* each other, and not on each other, that's victory. When we build each other and not destroy each other, that's victory. Red, yellow, brown, black and white—we're all precious in God's sight."

—Jesse L. Jackson

For God giveth to a man that is good in his sight wisdom, and knowledge, and joy. Ecclesiastes 2:26

As he viewed his ministry now, he did not dare preach without praying long for wisdom. He no longer thought of his dramatic delivery and its effect on his audience. The great question with him now was, "What would Jesus do?"

from *In His Steps*

Remind me, Lord Jesus, that what others

think of me isn't important. Peel off the

mask I wear to impress people. I can't do

this on my own, God—I need Your wisdom.

"Pure wisdom always directs itself towards God;

the purest wisdom is knowledge of God."

—Lew Wallace

What is that to thee? Follow thou me.   John 21:22

How much had the members of the First Church ever suffered in an attempt to imitate Jesus? Was Christian discipleship a thing of conscience simply, of custom, or tradition? Was it necessary in order to follow Jesus' steps to go up Calvary as well as the Mount of Transfiguration?

from *In His Steps*

Help me, Father, not to be a Christian simply

out of habit or because it's socially acceptable.

Show me how I need to change my life.

"It is easy to sing—'He will break every fetter' and at the same time be living a life of obvious slavery to yourself. Yielding to Jesus will break every form of slavery in any human life."

—Oswald Chambers

Whosoever he be of you that forsaketh not all that he

hath, he cannot be my disciple. Luke 14:33

"I want to do something that will cost me something in

the way of sacrifice. I am hungry to suffer something."

from *In His Steps*

Show me how to give You everything, Jesus, the good parts and the bad, the big things and the small.

"Adore Him in the midst of your weakness, offer yourself to Him from time to time, and when you hurt the most, ask Him humbly and lovingly (the way a child asks his father) to help you submit to His holy will."

—Brother Lawrence

And he that taketh not his cross, and followeth after

me, is not worthy of me. Matthew 10:38

"I have found my cross and it is a heavy one, but I

shall never be satisfied until I take it up and carry it."

from *In His Steps*

Give me Your strength,
Lord, so that I can
carry my cross.

"I have no one save the Holy Ghost to rely upon. My weak health and lack of ability seem to deny me success, but when I am weak, God is strong. Depending upon him alone, I go forward.. .."

—Kiye Sato Yamamuro

Righteousness shall go before him; and shall set us in

the way of his steps. Psalm 85:13

"What would Jesus do?" That question had become a

part of his whole life now. It was greater than any other.

from *In His Steps*

Let my entire life, dear Christ,
be focused on You. Be the center of my
thoughts, the center of my work,
the center of my love.

"Nothing will do except righteousness;

and no other concept of righteousness will

do, except Christ's."

—Matthew Arnold

Therefore if any man be in Christ, he is a new creature: old things are passed away; behold, all things are become new. 2 Corinthians 5:17

The transformation of these. . .lives into praying, rapturous lovers of Christ, struck Rachel and Virginia every time with the feeling that people may have had when they saw Lazarus walk out of the tomb.

from *In His Steps*

Thank You, my Lord,
for the new life springing up
in me—amazing,
wonder-filled, real.

"The experience of salvation means that in your actual life things are really altered, you no longer look at things as you used to; your desires are new, old things have lost their power."

—Oswald Chambers

Charge them that are rich in this world, that they be

not highminded, nor trust in uncertain riches, but in

the living God, who giveth us richly all things to enjoy;

That they do good, that they be rich in good works.

1 Timothy 6:17-18

"I have come to know lately that the money which I have called my own is not mine, but God's. If I, as a steward of His, see some wise way to invest His money, it is not an occasion for vainglory or thanks from anyone simply because I have proved honest in my administration of the funds He has asked me to use for His glory."

from *In His Steps*

Dear God, help me not to take pride in money. Help me not to worry about it either. Instead, remind me that my money now belongs to You.

"It is not the rich man only who is under the domination of things; they too are slaves who, having no money, are unhappy from the lack of it."

—George MacDonald

Seek ye first the kingdom of God, and his righteousness; and all these things shall be added unto you. Matthew 6:33

"If I shall, in the course of my obedience to my promise, meet with loss or trouble in the world, I can depend upon the genuine, practical sympathy and fellowship of any other Christian who has, with me, made the pledge to do all things by the rule, 'What would Jesus do?' "

from *In His Steps*

Thank You, Jesus, for taking care of me through Your Body, the Church.

"You are not alone, you are in the Church. . . . In that community you are sheltered and united with all those all over the world who believe in Christ."

—Hans Kung

As for me and my house, we will serve the LORD.   Joshua 24:15

Truly, a man's foes are they of his own household when the rule

of Jesus is obeyed by some and disobeyed by others. Jesus is a

great divider of life. One must walk parallel with Him or directly

across His way.

from *In His Steps*

· ·

Let me follow You, my Lord, no matter
what my family thinks, whether
they approve or disapprove.

· ·

"If you are humble, nothing will touch you, neither praise nor disgrace, because you know what you are."

—Mother Teresa

If any man serve me, let him follow me; and where I am, there shall also my servant be: if any man serve me, him will my Father honour.   John 12:26

But the people had lately had their deepest convictions touched. They had been living so long on their surface feelings that they had broken the surface, the people were convicted of the meaning of their discipleship.

from *In His Steps*

I want to serve only You,
Christ Jesus.
Make me Your disciple.

"Make me firm and steadfast in good works, and make me persevere in thy service, so that I may always live to please thee, Lord Jesus Christ."

—Clare of Assisi

Abide in me, and I in you. As the branch cannot bear fruit of itself, except it abide in the vine; no more can ye, except ye abide in me.   John 15:4

"The greatest question in all of human life is summed up when we ask, 'What would Jesus do?' if, as we ask it, we also try to answer it from a growth in knowledge of Jesus Himself. We must know Jesus before we can imitate Him."

from *In His Steps*

Show me Yourself, Jesus.
I want to get to
know You.

"We need neither skill nor science for going to God,

but only a heart determined to devote itself to nothing

except Him, for Him, loving Him only."

—Brother Lawrence

If ye keep my commandments, ye shall abide in my love; even as I have kept my Father's commandments, and abide in his love. These things have I spoken unto you, that my joy might remain in you, and that your joy might be full. John 15:10-11

What our churches need today more than anything else

is this factor of joyful suffering for Jesus in some form.

Suffering that does not eliminate, but does appear to

intensify, a positive and practical joy.

from *In His Steps*

Give me a positive, practical joy, God. Help me to live in Your love, so that Your joy will live in me.

"Lord, you are my joy and happiness,

the only treasure I have in this world."

—Margery Kempe

And whosoever doth not bear his cross, and come

after me, cannot be my disciple.   Luke 14:27

"Is the test of discipleship any less today than it

was in Jesus' time?"

from *In His Steps*

When I was a child, I used to imitate my parents.

They were the people I loved most, and I wanted

to act just like them. You are the Person I love

most now, Jesus, and I want to act like You.

"Endeavor to become as humble and simple as a little

child for the love of our Lord, in imitation of him. . . ."

—Jean-Pierre de Caussade

But what things were gain to me, those I counted loss for Christ. Philippians 3:7

"I know what this [pledge to follow in Jesus' steps] will mean to you and me. It will mean the complete change of very many habits. It will mean, possibly, social loss. It will mean very probably, in many cases, loss of money. It will mean suffering. It will mean what following Jesus meant in the first century, and then it meant suffering, loss, hardship. . . ."

from *In His Steps*

Jesus, help me to change my habits. Separate me from anything that will turn me toward myself and away from You.

"I live for my work;
For a good salary
which sustains a home of my own,
enough to eat out twice a week. . .
to enjoy holidays. . .
I live for my work;
It gives me a good reason for dressing up. . .
When I'm not working
there is nothing and no one
Only You, O God. . ."

—Kathy Keay

Now when Jesus heard these things, he said unto him, Yet lackest thou one thing: sell all that thou hast, and distribute unto the poor, and thou shalt have treasure in heaven: and come, follow me. And when he heard this, he was very sorrowful: for he was very rich. Luke 18:22–23

Our Christianity loves its ease and comfort too well to take up anything so rough and heavy as a cross.

from *In His Steps*

Help me, Father, not to
love my own comfort more
than I love You.

"When we are fully and wholly given up to the Lord, I am sure the heart can long for nothing so much as that our time, talents, life, soul, and spirit, may become upon earth a constant and living sacrifice."

—Lady Huntington, in a letter to John Wesley.

Lay not up for yourselves treasures upon earth, where moth and rust doth corrupt, and where thieves break through and steal: But lay up for yourselves treasures in heaven, where neither moth nor rust doth corrupt, and where thieves do not break through nor steal: For where your treasure is, there will your heart be also.

Matthew 6:19–21

What is the gain or loss of money compared with the unsearchable riches of eternal life which are beyond the reach of speculation, loss or change?

from *In His Steps*

Thank You, Jesus, that no matter what happens in my life, I am eternally safe.

"You, bravest lion, have burst through the heavens. You have destroyed death, and are building life in the golden city. Grant us society in that city, and let us dwell in You. . . ."

—Hildegard of Bingen

Then shalt thou understand righteousness, and judgment, and equity; yea, every good path. When wisdom entereth into thine heart, and knowledge is pleasant unto thy soul; Discretion shall preserve thee, understanding shall keep thee. Proverbs 2:9–11

"What would Jesus do?" Felicia prayed and hoped and worked and regulated her life by the answer to that question. It was the inspiration of her conduct and the answer to all her ambition.

from *In His Steps*

May Your love,
Christ, regulate
my life.

"Christ has no body now on earth but yours;

yours are the only hands with which He can do His work,

yours are the only feet with which He can go about the world,

yours are the only eyes through which His compassion

can shine forth upon a troubled world.

Christ has no body on earth now but yours."

—Teresa of Avila

And whosoever shall give to drink unto one of these little ones a cup of cold water only in the name of a disciple, verily I say unto you, he shall in no wise lose his reward. Matthew 10:42

Men would give money that would not think of giving themselves. And the money they gave did not represent any real sacrifice because they did not miss it. They gave what was easiest to give, what hurt them the least. Where did the sacrifice come in? Was this following Jesus? Was this going with Him all the way?

from *In His Steps*

Jesus, I want to go with You all the way—even if it hurts.

"If he does not come in close contact with them, he cannot know who the poor are. . . . He gives not only his money but also his time. He could have spent both his money and time on himself, but he wanted to spend himself instead."

—Mother Teresa

There is no man that hath left house, or parents, or brethren, or wife, or children, for the kingdom of God's sake, Who shall not receive manifold more in this present time, and in the world to come life everlasting. Luke 18:29-30

His decision to live a life of personal sacrifice. . .was not a new idea. It was an idea started by Jesus Christ when He left His Father's House and forsook the riches that were His in order to get nearer humanity and, by becoming a part of its sin, helping to draw humanity apart from its sin.

from *In His Steps*

Let me, like You, Lord, leave myself behind so that I can get close enough to others to show them Your love.

"In order to survive, love has to be nourished by sacrifices. The words of Jesus, 'Love one another as I have loved you,' must be not only a light to us but a flame that consumes the self in us."

—Mother Teresa

For whosoever will save his life shall lose it: and whosoever will lose his life for my sake shall find it. For what is a man profited, if he shall gain the whole world, and lose his own soul? or what shall a man give in exchange for his soul?

Matthew 16:25–26

Where was suffering to come in unless there was an actual self-denial of some sort? And what was to make that self-denial apparent to themselves or anyone else, unless it took this concrete, actual, personal form of trying to share the deepest suffering and sin of the city?

from *In His Steps*

God, help me to deny myself in concrete, personal ways.

"Give all you have, as well as all you are,

a spiritual sacrifice to him who withheld

not from you his Son, his only Son. . . ."

—John Wesley

Howbeit when he, the Spirit of truth, is come, he will guide you into all truth: for he shall not speak of himself; but whatsoever he shall hear, that shall he speak: and he will shew you things to come. John 16:13

Will the Church. . .respond to the call to follow Him? Will it choose to walk in His steps of pain and suffering? Grieve [the Holy Spirit] not, O city! For He was never more ready to revolutionize this world than now!

from *In His Steps*

Help me, dear Lord, to hear the Spirit's voice speaking in my life.

"Just as transparent substances, when subjected to the light, themselves glitter and give off light, so does the soul, illumined by the Holy Spirit, give light to others. . . ."

—St. Basil

We then that are strong ought to bear the infirmities of the weak, and not to please ourselves. Romans 15:1

What was the trouble with the world? It was suffering from selfishness. No one ever lived who had succeeded in overcoming selfishness like Jesus.

from *In His Steps*

● ●

I understand now, Jesus: Sin is just another name for

selfishness. Remind me that whenever I put myself at

the center of my life, then You cannot live in me.

● ●

"Sin is a tree with a great many branches, but it has

only one root, namely, the inordinate love of self."

—Kirby Page

Then shall ye call upon me, and ye shall go and pray unto me, and I will hearken unto you. And ye shall seek me, and find me, when ye shall search for me with all your heart. And I will be found of you, saith the LORD.   Jeremiah 29:12–14

Was the church then so far from the Master that the people no longer found Him in the church?

from *In His Steps*

Father, bring the Church back to You, so that it can truly be Your body.

"When religion goes wrong it is because, in one form

or another, men have made the mistake of trying to

turn to God without turning away from the self."

—Aelred Graham

But what things were gain to me, those I counted loss for Christ. Yea doubtless, and I count all things but loss for the excellency of the knowledge of Christ Jesus my Lord: for whom I have suffered the loss of all things. Philippians 3:7-8

"Are the Christians of America ready to have their discipleship tested? How about the men who possess large wealth? Are they ready to take that wealth and use it as Jesus would? How about the men and women of great wealth? Are they ready to consecrate that talent to humanity as Jesus undoubtedly would do?"

from *In His Steps*

Help me, Jesus, to give everything to You: my money, my possessions, my talents, my time, my love.

"Employ whatever God has entrusted you

with, in doing good, all possible good, in

every possible kind and degree. . . ."

—John Wesley

He that saith he abideth in him ought himself also so to walk, even as he walked. 1 John 2:6

"Would it not be true that if every Christian in America did as Jesus would do, society itself, the business world, yes, the very political system under which our commercial and governmental activity is carried on, would be so changed that human suffering would be reduced to a minimum?"

from *In His Steps*

Use me, Christ,
to change
my world.

"Help me, Lord, to remember that religion is not to be confined to the church. . . ,nor exercised only in prayer and meditation, but that everywhere I am in Thy Presence."

—Susanna Wesley

My grace is sufficient for thee: for my strength is made perfect in weakness. 2 Corinthians 12:9

"There is a great quantity of nominal Christianity today. There is need of more of the real kind. We need revival of the Christianity of Christ."

from *In His Steps*

We need revival, God. Please begin that revival by sending Your Spirit to bring my own heart back to life.

"You take the bare fields, bleak and desolate, and

dress them in green, splashing us with colors,

reminding us that Life comes through You."

—Tammy Felton

Let us not love in word, neither in tongue;

but in deed and in truth.

1 John 3:18

"If our definition of being a Christian is simply to enjoy the privileges of worship, be generous at no expense to ourselves, have a good, easy time surrounded by pleasant friends and by comfortable things, live respectably and at the same time avoid the world's great stress of sin and trouble because it is too much pain to bear it—if this is our definition of Christianity, surely we are a long way from following the steps of Him who trod the way with groans and tears and sobs of anguish for a lost humanity; who sweat, as it were, great drops of blood, who cried out on the upreared cross, 'My God, my God, why hast thou forsaken me?' "

from *In His Steps*

• •

Dear Jesus, You loved me enough to experience pain, both

physical and emotional. You didn't draw the line and say,

"No more, I've given all I can." No, You gave everything, even

Your life. Please fill me with that same kind of love.

• •

"The law of love can never be a cherishing of self at

the expense of the loved one, but must always be the

cherishing of the loved one at the expense of self."

—Hannah Whitall Smith

That ye might walk worthy of the Lord unto all pleasing, being fruitful in every good work, and increasing in the knowledge of God; Strengthened with all might, according to his glorious power, unto all patience and longsuffering with joyfulness. Colossians 1:10–11

"What is it to be a Christian? It is to imitate Jesus. It is to do as He would do. It is to walk in His steps."

from *In His Steps*

· ·

I can remember when I was little, walking behind my mother

through the snow, trying to put my feet into each one of her

footprints. Help me now, Jesus, to do the same with You. I want

to walk in Your steps.

· ·

"If you look for anything but more love, you are looking

wide of the mark, you are getting out of the royal way."

—John Wesley

Our heart is not turned back, neither have our steps declined from thy way.

Psalm 44:18

"Where He leads me I will follow,

Where He leads me I will follow,

Where He leads me I will follow,

I'll go with Him, with Him all the way!"

from *In His Steps*

We're playing "Follow the Leader," Lord. You lead, I'll follow.

"God will lead you as if by the hand, if

only you do not doubt, and are filled with

love for Him rather than fear for yourself."

—Francois de Fenelon

Behold, I make all things new. Revelation 21:5

Truly, this man in Christ was a new creature. Old

things were passed away. Behold, all things in

him had become new.

from *In His Steps*

Thank You, Jesus, for making me new, over and over, morning by morning.

"I have come upon the happy discovery that this life

hid with Christ in God is a continuous unfolding."

—Eugenia Price

Thou wilt shew me the path of life: in thy presence is fulness of joy; at thy right hand there are pleasures for evermore. Psalm 16:11

"Just as I am, without one plea,

But that Thy blood was shed for me,

And that Thou bidst me come to Thee,

O Lamb of God, I come, I come."

from *In His Steps*

"Just as I am, thou wilt receive,

Wilt welcome, pardon, cleanse, relieve,

Because Thy promise I believe,

O Lamb of God, I come, I come."

from *In His Steps*

Father, I'm glad You take me the way I am. You love me with all my flaws—I don't have to make myself good before You'll receive me. Instead, You welcome me now, and I know Your love will make me clean and whole.

"God can make you anything. . .but you

have to put everything into His hands."

—Mahalia Jackson

My sheep hear my voice, and I know them, and they follow me: And I give unto them eternal life; and they shall never perish, neither shall any man pluck them out of my hand.   John 10:27-28

"Let us follow Jesus closer; let us walk in His steps where it will cost us something more than it is costing us now."

from *In His Steps*

Help me, Christ, to walk in Your steps—even when it costs me something.

"When he asks for and receives our all, he gives in return that which is above price—his own presence. The price is not great when compared with what he gives in return; it is our blindness and unwillingness to yield that make it seem great."

—Rosalind Goforth

Teach me, O LORD, the way of thy statutes; and I shall keep it unto the end.

Psalm 119:33

"Suppose that the church membership generally in this country made this

pledge and lived up to it! What a revolution it would cause in Christendom!"

from *In His Steps*

Start the revolution,
my Lord, in
my own life.

" 'Love thy neighbor' is a precept

which could transform the world

if it were universally practiced."

—Mary McLeod Bethune

For the poor shall never cease out of the land: therefore I command thee, saying, Thou shalt open thine hand wide unto thy brother, to thy poor, and to thy needy, in thy land. Deuteronomy 15:11

"What have I done with God's money all these years but gratify my own selfish personal desires? What can I do with the rest of it but try to make some reparation for what I have stolen from God?"

from *In His Steps*

I don't want to steal from You any longer, God. Show me how to give back to You the money with which You've entrusted me.

"You cannot love money and your brethren

at the same time."

—Emmanuel Suhard

But seek ye first the kingdom of God, and his righteousness; and all these things shall be added unto you. Matthew 6:33

"We were not to ask any question about 'Will it pay?' but all our action was to be based on the one question, 'What would Jesus do?'"

from *In His Steps*

Show me how to assess my actions in Your light, Jesus, rather than in the dark of my own selfishness.

"We ought to change the legend on our money from 'In God We Trust' to 'In Money We Trust.' Because, as a nation, we've got far more faith in money these days than we do in God."

—Arthur Hoppe

For he shall deliver the needy when he crieth; the poor also, and him that hath no helper. He shall spare the poor and needy, and shall save the souls of the needy. Psalm 72:12–13

"Is it possible you can go your ways careless or thoughtless of the awful condition of men and women and children who are dying, body and soul, for need of Christian help? Can you say this is none of your business?"

from *In His Steps*

Remind me, God,
what my business here
on earth really is.

"Business! . . . Mankind was my business. The common welfare was my business; charity, mercy, forebearance, and benevolence were, all, my business. The dealings of my trade were but a drop of water in the comprehensive ocean of my business!"

—Charles Dickens (Marley's Ghost)